Eat at Joe's

Written by Sharon Wohl
Illustrated by Lesley Grainger

Creator of The Phonics Game™

Printed in the U.S.A.

A Better Way of Learning • www.phonicsgame.com

Pete likes to eat.
He sits on a chair.
He waits to get a meal.

Pete has chips and dip on a plate.
Pete eats chips and dip, chips and dip.
Pete yells, "No! I hate stale chips."

Kate has fresh chips on a plate.
Pete eats the chips.
Kate smiles.

Pete has a glass.
"This needs ice," he yells.
Kate adds ice to the glass.
Kate smiles.

"I can't sit on this chair," yells Pete.
Kate has a spare chair.
She smiles.

The meat is on Pete's plate.
Pete takes a bite.
He yells, "No! This is not hot."

The meat is on the stove.
The meat is back on Pete's plate.
It is hot.
Pete eats the meat.
Kate smiles.

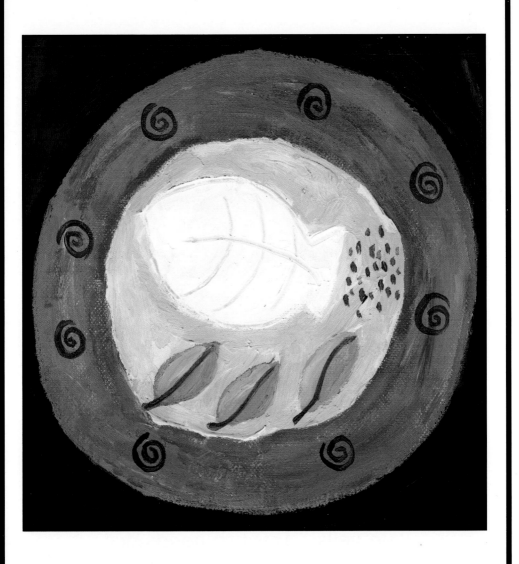

"I like fish with bay leaves,
chives and dill," yells Pete.
Kate has fish on a plate.

Pete yells, "This fish needs dill.
I can't eat this fish!"
Kate smiles and adds dill to the fish.
Pete eats the fish.

Kate has pie in a dish.
Pete yells, "I need ice cream
on this pie!"

Kate smiles and adds ice cream to the dish.
Pete eats the pie and ice cream.

Kate has tea in a cup.
Pete sips the tea.
"No! This tea is weak!
I can't drink this tea."

Kate smiles.
She has five tea bags.
Pete sips his tea.

Kate has a check with tax
and hands it to Pete.
"No, I can't pay!" yells Pete.

"I quit," yells Kate,
and she runs to the street.
Kate rests and smiles.